Ha Ha Hyena

Written by
Alan Durant

Illustrated by
Dynamo

Hyena loved to laugh. Most of all, he loved to laugh at others.

"Ha ha! Aren't you long and lanky!" he laughed at Giraffe.

"Ha ha! Aren't you fat and flabby!" he sniggered at Hippo.

"Ha ha! Haven't you got a great big nose!" he jibed at Elephant.

"Ha ha! Look at your curly ginger hair!" he sniped at Lion.

"Ha ha! Aren't you spotty?" he jeered at Leopard.

Day after day, Hyena laughed and sniggered, jibed and jeered at the other animals.

The other animals all tried to ignore Hyena's insults. Finally they had had enough.

"You're so rude," grumbled Elephant. "I'm going to splash you with my trunk."

He dipped his trunk into the river and blew out a huge spray of water.

But Hyena hid under the big leaves of an umbrella tree.

"Ha, ha, big nose! Can't soak me!" he laughed.

"I'm going to squash you," rumbled Hippo. He plodded out of the river and chased Hyena, but Hyena ran round and round until Hippo was tired and dizzy.

"Ha, ha, fatso! Can't squash me!" Hyena laughed.

"I'm going to throw you up into the sky," groused Giraffe.

But Hyena squashed himself flat against the ground, so that Giraffe couldn't reach him.

"Ha, ha, lanky! You can't throw me!" he laughed.

"I'm going to bite your bottom," snarled Lion.

He leapt at Hyena, but Hyena dodged him and Lion banged his head on a big rock.

"Ha, ha, ginger! You can't bite me!" he laughed.

The animals were fed up.

"Why don't you chase him, Leopard?" they said. "You're the fastest. You could catch him and teach him a lesson."

But Leopard shook his head. "I'll teach him a lesson, but I'm not going to chase him," he growled.

"Then what will you do?" asked the others.

"You can't insult Hyena. He doesn't care what name you call him."

"Well that may be," agreed Leopard, "but I have a plan …"

The next day, when Hyena met Lion, as usual he made fun of his mane.

This time Lion didn't frown or growl. He smiled a big toothy smile.

"Hey, thank you, Hyena," he purred, preening himself. "I've been combing my mane all morning. I'm so glad you like it."

"Eh?" barked Hyena. He shrugged and walked away.

Next Hyena met Giraffe.

"Hi, lanky neck! Ha ha!" he sneered.

"Why, thank you, Hyena. I believe my neck *has* grown," Giraffe replied, stretching up high. "I can see further than ever."

"What?" barked Hyena. He giggled a bit and pattered away.

"Hey, big nose! Ha ha!" Hyena called when he saw Elephant.

"Thank you, Hyena," boomed Elephant. "It's so kind of you to notice. See what a loud noise it can make." He lifted his trunk and went "Trump! Trump! Trump!"

"Ugh!" muttered Hyena and he ran off away.

Hyena trotted down to the river.

"Hey, fatso!" he shouted to Hippo. "What a wibbly wobbly lump you are. Ha ha!"

"Quite so, Hyena! Look what I can do!" Hippo bellowed. He stood up and wobbled his big belly like a giant jelly.

Hyena gave a little laugh and plodded away.

Hyena found Leopard, lying under a tree.

"Hey, spotty!" he greeted him. "What a spotty botty you've got. Ha ha!" he mocked. But Leopard just grinned. "I'm so pleased you think so, Hyena. Thank you very much." Leopard chuckled, shaking his bottom this way and that, until the spots made Hyena quite giddy.

Hyena didn't know what to say. He slunk away and sat on a grassy mound in the sun.

Hyena was puzzled. What was going on?
Suddenly he heard a noise behind him and turned to see the other animals gathered there. They pointed at him and laughed.

"Ha ha, Hyena!" they declared together. "What a silly thing to do, trying to make fun of us like that!"

Hyena frowned. He looked upset.
Leopard came up to him.
"That was a good joke we played on you, wasn't it, Hyena?" he grinned.

Hyena thought about this – and he thought a bit more. It *was* a good joke, he decided, Leopard was right … and then Hyena started to laugh too!

Now all the animals laughed and chuckled and giggled together.

From that day on, Hyena never laughed at the other animals or called them names.

But he loved to laugh *with* them often – and that made everyone, including Hyena, much, much happier.